THiS BOOK
BELONGS TO:
_____

To my Grandma for making my
childhood magical, one pickle jar at a time.

- M.S.

First edition published in 2021 by Flying Eye Books, an imprint
of Nobrow Ltd. 27 Westgate Street, London, E8 3RL.

Text and illustrations © Martin Stanev 2021.

Martin Stanev has asserted his right under the Copyright, Designs and Patents Act,
1988, to be identified as the Author and Illustrator of this Work.

3 5 7 9 10 8 6 4 2

Published in the US by Nobrow (US) Inc.
Printed in Poland on FSC certified paper.

ISBN: 978-1-838740-18-4
www.flyingeyebooks.com

Martin Stanev

THE PLANET IN A PICKLE JAR

Flying Eye Books

Our Grandma lived a lonely and quiet life.

She saved up all her words and smiles
for when we came to visit.

She cooked boring meals.

And told the longest stories.

Her house was as dull and ordinary as she was.

All she did was shop,

knit,

and make jars of pickles.

She never did anything fun.

One evening, Grandma wanted to tell us something important, so we tried to look interested.

Children, our world is very fragile. If we don't do anything to preserve it, it will slowly fade away...

until all that is left is concrete, smoke and dust.

For once, we listened.

That night, we gazed at the world outside,
thinking about Grandma's words.

Suddenly, a star fell from the sky and vanished.

Were things already
starting to fade away?

We rushed to ask Grandma,
only to find she'd vanished too.

Grandma?

We searched high and low, but all we could find was . . .

AARRHHH!

Searching for a place to hide,
we discovered a mysterious door leading
down some stairs we'd never seen before.

We hurried inside, hoping they would lead us to Grandma.

Suddenly, we heard something at the end of the corridor.

After what felt like a lifetime,
we emerged into the most incredible room.
It was a huge sanctuary. Had our Grandma
built this? Maybe she wasn't so boring after all . . .

HEEELP!

. . . and right now, she needed our help!

We squeezed her close, glad that she hadn't vanished
like the star and everything else in her story.

I do want to keep preserving
all the beautiful things on our
planet for your futures, but I'm
afraid I'm getting old now.

I think it might be time
I had a little help...

So that's what we did.

We began helping our Grandma to preserve the
wonders of our planet, one pickle jar at a time.